Ben's Christmas Carol

by **Toby Forward**

illustrated by **Ruth Brown**

DUTTON CHILDREN'S BOOKS ✶ New York

Text copyright © 1996 by Toby Forward
Illustrations copyright © 1996 by Ruth Brown

Published in the United States 1996 by Dutton Children's Books,
a division of Penguin Books USA Inc.
375 Hudson Street, New York, New York 10014
Originally published in Great Britain 1996 by Andersen Press, Ltd., London
Typography by Julia Goodman
Printed in Italy   First American Edition
ISBN 0-525-45593-0
4 6 8 10 9 7 5 3

For all Christmas mice

T.F.

For Bryony, Leonie, and Helena

R.B.

When the wind snapped cold and the icicles hung like sharks' teeth from the guttering, Tim snuffled along the baseboard and rubbed his poor cold paws together. He wondered whether Christmas would bring him anything at all this year.

When the great pine tree towered in the dining room and the logs crackled in the grate, Ben smoothed his whiskers and sniffed the air, relishing the thought of good things to come. He knew his belly soon would be full and fit.

On Christmas Eve, Tim stood waiting in that secret place of mice, the dark tunnel behind the walls where cats cannot stalk and dogs cannot run. Soon he heard Ben coming toward him, dragging something that sounded big and juicy.

"Merry Christmas, Ben," said Tim, holding out a box tied with a red ribbon.

Ben sucked in his cheeks. "Bah," he said. "It's all the same to me, whatever day it is." And off he went, dragging his plum behind him, not even pausing to accept the gift that Tim still held.

"That looked like a mighty nice plum." Tim sighed and turned for home.

As Ben snuggled down into his cozy comforter, he remembered the meeting in the passageway. "Christmas," he said to himself scornfully. "It's just another day." But he tossed and turned that night, even though Tim slept soundly, far away in his own room.

"Don't you know why you can't sleep?" said a thin and whispery voice.

"Who's there?" Ben nearly jumped out of his fur. A tiny white mouse was peering through the frosty windowpane. "Go away," said Ben.

"Don't you want company? It's Christmas Eve," the visitor replied.

"Bah," said Ben. "It's all the same to me. But you may as well come in."

The little white mouse opened the window and scrambled through. He was cold and thin, thinner even than Tim. Immediately he went and stood by the dying embers of the fire. "Ahhh," he said. "Warmth at last. That's better."

"Careful," said Ben. "You're blocking the heat from me."

"Sorry, Ben," said the little mouse sadly, moving aside.

"How do you know my name? And who are you?"

"My name is Jacob," said the white mouse. "You can call me Jake." But he did not answer Ben's other question. "That's a very nice plum you have."

"It's mine," said Ben, quickly moving to lock the plum in his cabinet. "For Christmas."

"I thought you didn't bother with all that," said Jake.

"Well," said Ben. "I don't. But it's the only time of year I can find candied plums. And there is nothing better in the world than a plum."

"Nothing?" said Jake.

"Nothing," said Ben firmly.

"I once would have agreed with you, Ben. But now I know better," said Jake. "I will bet you that I can find three others who, like me, want something more than a candied plum tonight."

Ben found this rather interesting. "What if you're wrong and I win? You're poor and have nothing to give me."

"I can help you sleep," said Jake promptly.

"And if I lose?"

"The plum is mine."

Ben looked at his bed. The sheets were tangled and twisted. The pillow was surely cold by now. And, besides, it was a sure bet. Who wouldn't want a plum?

So, Ben wrapped up warmly, taking his plum—for safekeeping, of course—
and they set off into the night. Jake led Ben through a long alleyway, across a
cobbled yard, and down a short flight of stone steps.

There, in a damp, dark cellar, a Christmas celebration was going on. "How can they be so happy?" Ben wondered aloud. "They are so poor and thin." The little mice inside had ragged clothes, like Jake's and Tim's, and the table was spread with only a few grains of rice. But still it was the merriest party Ben had ever seen.

As they entered the room,
one young mouse noticed them immediately.
His eyes grew big and round when he saw what Ben carried.

"Here's your first test," Jake urged. "Go on. Tell him you'll
give him the plum if he'll leave the party and spend Christmas on his own."

Ben approached the merrymakers.

"Is that a candied plum?" the young mouse asked. "I've never really seen
one before, but I hear there's nothing so good in all the world."

"It's yours," said Ben.

"Oh, thank you! I'll share it with the others."

"No—you must leave and eat it all alone. That is the condition," said Ben.

The little mouse looked around. "That's not a good condition. I'd rather
be with the others, even without the plum." And he scurried back to join
the dancing.

"Come away," said Jake. And Ben followed him, but not without a glance
over his shoulder at the children and a strange feeling in his heart.

Next, Jake took Ben to an old inn.
The ceilings were low, and the beams
were black from the fire that was ever-
burning in the hearth.

A crowd of mice were just raising their glasses and drinking a toast. "To Christmas!" they cried.

Ben wished he had a glass to raise and took a nibble at his plum.

"Careful," warned Jake, "or it will all be gone." Then, as though a glass had magically appeared in his hand, he lifted his paw into the air. "To Ben!" he cried. But the other mice put their glasses down on the table.

"I won't drink to him," said the oldest mouse. "It would spoil Christmas."

Ben's eyes filled with tears.

"Offer him the plum," Jake said.

Ben crept over and whispered in the blind old mouse's ear. "Do you like plums?"

"I love them," said the mouse.

"If I give you this one, will you drink to Ben's health?"

The old man did not recognize Ben's voice. "No, I won't," he said. "That mean mouse doesn't deserve a Christmas toast."

Jake gently took Ben's arm. "Now come away."

As they crossed the cobbled yard in front of Ben's house, Ben felt
very cross. "Well, that's only two," he said. "I win. Now help me get to sleep."

But Jake said not a word as they scurried inside and across the big room, where
the great tree held its branches over their heads and the parcels lay ready for morn-
ing. Ben twitched his whiskers in greedy excitement as they passed.

Behind the walls, in the secret place of mice where cats cannot stalk and dogs
cannot run, Jake led Ben down a dark passage.

"This isn't the way," said Ben. But Jake led on, all the way to Tim's room.

Inside, there was no fire burning in the grate. A tattered blanket made of newspaper was the only covering on the bed. And a little box, tied with a red ribbon, lay on the floor.

"I've never been here before," said Ben. "Why does he keep it so cold? Is he asleep? We might wake him up."

"No, we won't," said Jake.

Ben touched Tim's shoulder. "He's awfully cold," said Ben. "And so thin." Tim had not moved. "Is he all right?"

"Look in the parcel, Ben," said Jake. "It was meant for you."

Ben picked up the box and read the label aloud. "To Ben: Merry Christmas, from Tim." He pulled the red ribbon and opened the lid. "Why, it's a grape," he announced. He reached over to touch Tim's shoulder again, but instead let his hand fall. He looked around the bleak, empty room, and then he looked down at the thin, cold, still figure.

"Was it all he had?"

"Let's go back now," said Jake. "I'll let you sleep."

"I'll leave him the plum," Ben decided.

"Oh, he won't want it now," said Jake. "Remember? I said there were three who would not."

"Why?" cried Ben. "Why has this happened?"

"Think of the party," said Jake. "Think of the old mouse at the inn."

"He said I was a mean mouse," said Ben. He looked at Tim one last time. "So this is my fault. I let this happen."

Ben's room was still warm and cozy. The embers glowed in the grate. The bedclothes were turned back. Ben's presents to himself lay under the twig.

"I won't sleep," said Ben, as he snuggled down in bed. "I really won't. Poor Tim. Isn't there any way we can make him all right? Can it really be too late?"

Jake pulled the covers up to Ben's chin. And Ben fell fast asleep.

Suddenly, the bells were ringing. The sun was gleaming bright
and cold in the frosty air. The icicles hung like jewels in the
light. Ben jumped out of his bed and tripped on the plum. He
began to shout in anger and then stopped, put his paw to his
mouth, and remembered.

Ben picked up the plum and scurried pell-mell down the tunnel. He burst into Tim's room, but Tim was lying quite still in the bed. The room was cold.

Then, as the door slammed back, Tim yawned and stretched. "Merry Christmas, Ben," he said. Ben jumped into the air in delight and nearly knocked Tim out of bed as he hurled himself and the plum at the little mouse.

"Merry Christmas!" he shouted.

"For me?"

"Yes! And more! Lots more!"

Tim gave Ben the parcel with the red ribbon. "It seems to have unwrapped itself in the night," he said. "I'm sorry."

"I don't want it," said Ben. "Keep it!"

"But, please," said Tim. "It's your present."

"I mean—it's the best grape in all the world!" cried Ben, laughing at himself. "Now come with me!"

Ben dragged Tim down the tunnel, stopping at his own room to gather up the presents from under the twig. Then he led Tim outside and down the steps, and together they ran to the party.

"Merry Christmas!" shouted Ben as they entered.

The mice looked surprised, and more than a little bit frightened when they saw Ben, but they cheered up when Tim looked over his shoulder.

"Merry Christmas!" they all called back.

So, Ben spread his offerings on the table, and shoveled all the coal on the fire at once and called out to the other mice to run to his house and fill their buckets. And they did, and the room was hot and bright, and the dancing was fast. And the laughter was loud.

Ben spied the old mouse from the inn and put a glass into his hand. "Merry Christmas!" he said.

"To Ben!" said Tim. And the others all called out, "To Ben!" The old mouse hesitated at first. But then he raised his glass to his lips, and Ben beamed with pride.

When everyone had tired out, and the little ones were snoozing and the older ones were blinking sleep from their eyes, Ben and Tim went home, arm in arm.

They walked together through the dark tunnel behind the walls, the secret place of mice where cats cannot stalk and dogs cannot run.

"Merry Christmas," said Tim as he reached his door.

Carefully—oh, so carefully—Ben said, "Won't you come to my place for one last drink and a warm before you go?"

"But I've never really been there," said Tim.
"Will you always come to see me now?"
"Yes, please," said Tim.
"It's not too late, is it?" asked Ben.
"Never too late," said Tim.

This book is inspired by *A Christmas Carol*, the famous tale of the haunting of Ebenezer Scrooge. Charles Dickens wrote the story in 1843, when he was only thirty-one. He hoped it would move the public to take better care of impoverished children, for he had witnessed the hard lives of many young people and had himself been neglected as a child. Published in November of that year, the first edition met with tremendous success and sold out by Chistmas Eve. Ever since, generations of children and adults have been touched by Dickens' unforgettable holiday present to the world, originally subtitled *A Ghost Story of Christmas*.

CHARLES DICKENS

Toby Forward lives in Yorkshire, England, with his wife and their two daughters. His novel *Traveling Backward* is available in the United States from Puffin Books.

Ruth Brown is an extremely popular illustrator whose numerous books for children have garnered praise and awards from many quarters. She is most known for her talents at rendering beautiful, naturalistic animals and her moody, evocative settings. *Publishers Weekly* called her recent book, *Copycat*, "as comfortable and familiar as a beloved pet." *School Library Journal* claimed, in a starred review, that *The Picnic* was "a must for all picture-book shelves." Ms. Brown lives in Bath, England.